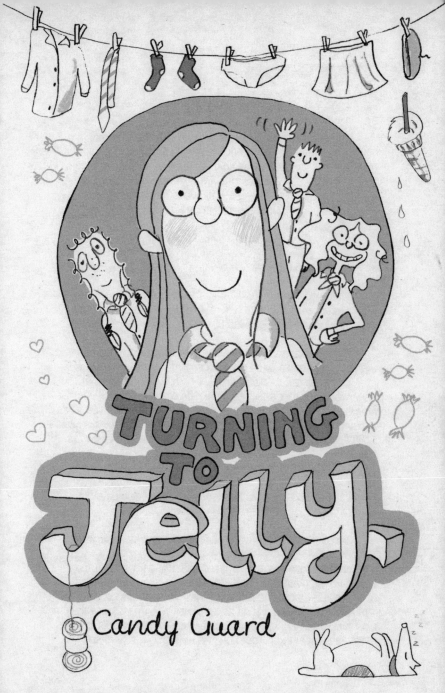

TURNING TO Jelly

Candy Guard

MACMILLAN CHILDREN'S BOOKS

FIRST PUBLISHED 2014 BY MACMILLAN CHILDREN'S BOOKS
A DIVISION OF MACMILLAN PUBLISHERS LIMITED
20 NEW WHARF ROAD, LONDON N1 9RR
BASINGSTOKE AND OXFORD
ASSOCIATED COMPANIES THROUGHOUT THE WORLD
WWW.PANMACMILLAN.COM

ISBN 978-1-4472-5610-6

135798642

A CIP CATALOGUE RECORD FOR THIS BOOK IS AVAILABLE FROM
THE BRITISH LIBRARY.

PRINTED AND BOUND BY CPI GROUP (UK) LTD, CROYDON CR0 4YY

For my mum and brothers,
for being funny

-1-
Minor Details

Myf, Roobs and I have tried on our new uniforms 34 times, because `TOMORROW` we start **B**ig **S**chool (population 1,310). We are very **NERVOUS**, not least because my brother Jay says that, as we're new girls, we might get our heads flushed down the toilet . . .

. . . especially in those berets!

I was already a tad worried about my beret because Mum had knitted it for me,

BUT we knew it was part of the uniform because Myf had seen it in the ...

UNIFORM GUIDE

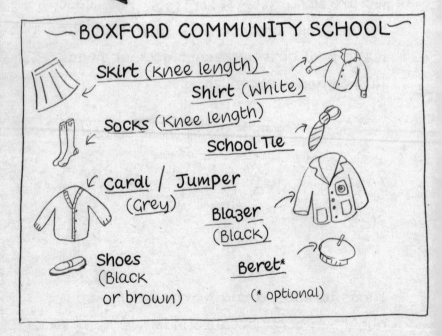

BOXFORD COMMUNITY SCHOOL

Skirt (Knee length)

Shirt (White)

Socks (Knee length)

School Tie

Cardi / Jumper (Grey)

Blazer (Black)

Shoes (Black or brown)

Beret*

(* optional)

Out of the 1,310 pupils at the school I will know —

 My brother, Jay

 Rubi Mistri ('Roobs')

Members of

 Myfanwy Hughes ('Myf')

The Faithful Club

 Ricky Chin (boy next door)

 Cicily Fanshaw (sporty smuggins)

Bethany Iceland
(ex-friend, now cool girl)

Roger Lovely (brother's friend, kept back 2 years for being ~~handsome~~ slow)
(my secret crush)

3

We were in my bedroom, AKA the temporary headquarters of The Faithful Club, having our weekly meeting. Ricky Chin from next door was only an associate member (boy) and wasn't listening, being more interested in taunting our dog, Fatty, with a cheesy whatsit.

We were discussing how to raise funds for the O.M.G. concert next year.

We started our gang,

THE FAITHFUL CLUB,

two years ago at primary school. We had badges (FC), a shed (or did have till Julian took it over as his aromatherapy home office) and even a SONG.

We are the Faithfullons, ♫ 🎵
   Often known as champions.
We live off Heinz baked beans;
   Our uniform is jeans.
We never do complain,
   But say again and AGAIN,
We are the Faithful,   ♫
   'aithful – o – O – ons!   ♪

We are . . .
la la la !
(doesn't know
words)

Ricky Chin
(boy)

5

Some of the minor details in the song weren't _EXACTLY_ true . . .

Myf didn't like baked beans . . .

Eeugh! All mushy!

Jeans always went up my bum and I **NEVER** wore them . . .

And Rubi was **ALWAYS** moaning . . .

And we weren't exactly **CHAMPIONS** at **ANYTHING**, except Myfanwy, who is champion at having the most hopscotch stones in her pencil case and knowing all 31 of them by name.

Toby

Jason

Crunch

Toffee

Gary

Sally

Alan

Dot

5

4

2

3

1

MYFANWY

just doesn't care!

7

RUBI on the other hand does care...

She is a terrible worrier.

She likes her uniform to be very neat

and gets upset if her mum irons her pleats all wonky.

What if?

She is very organised and clever.

She is very good at her schoolwork

☆ 10/10

BUT
she has
an overactive
imagination...

She's quite mean with money

My owes me 1p

but very kind.

... and sees potential disaster in every situation, for example she will think, 'Oh look at that beautiful stained-glass window!' and THEN think, 'What if I accidentally fell against it and it broke and I fell 30 feet to my death?'

Consequently she can be a bit of a KILLJOY.

And then there's me, Jelly (I'll explain about the stupid name later). I'm a **BIT** like Myfanwy and a **BIT** like Rubi . . .

Oh yes, and Ricky Chin is our token boy.

We make quite a good team, but I'd begun to **WORRY** that since we're starting Big School maybe it was a bit childish and **embarrassing** to have a **CLUB**.

I don't care if it IS 'barrassing.

Maybe it IS a bit embarrassing?

FC

FC

So we decided that as long as we only did it in our bedrooms (or shed, when we got it back), who would know?

But it wasn't only that worrying me – Jay kept saying things like 'You're such a baby! They'll make mincemeat of you at Big School!' and laughing at my taste in music and the way I speak and my clothes.

All his girlfriends have been very cool and grown up (unlike him) so I have been studying their clothes and way of speaking . . .

. . . to ensure I don't end up as mincemeat.

(Myf and Roobs are doomed, I'm afraid.)

-2-
Beret Embarrassing

The next day, stomachs akimbo, we all got the bus together, and Röger Lövely was on it!

He said I looked 'very smart',

but I DID notice him looking at my beret a bit PUNNILY.

It turned out that Jay was half right. We DIDN'T get our heads flushed down the toilet but our berets DID cause a lot of hilarity outside the school gates.

No one wore them, and hasn't since  1937

Everyone had a field day laughing and being mean . . .

Hur, hur!

Bon jaw!

D'you think it's the berets?

I don't care.

It was a bit of a shaky start but L**U**CKILY Myf, Roobs and I were all in the same class so we could :Cling: together.

13

Our form teacher is a very strange woman called Miss Haddock, who does actually look like a haddock, and is also the GAMES teacher.

Good morning, class 7H. Welcome to the team!

She made us all say our names one by one, which was quite scary, especially for me . . . 'Jelly' as you may have guessed, is my nickname. My real name is Roberta Rowntree, and Rowntree's are famous makers of jelly — my granny used to let us eat the jelly cubes.

She said they were good for our bones.

Just add hot (WATER) . . .

Well, what would YOU rather be called?

 **JELLY?**

Which sounds like I'm:

A) Wobbly
(only slightly when Röger Lövely is near
or I have to read aloud in French)

B) Slightly actually wobbly
(Things jiggle when I run)

C) Brightly coloured
(when I run, am near Röger Lövely,
have to read aloud in French – or if
I'm really unlucky all 3 at once)

Je m'appelle . . .

or...

Roberta?

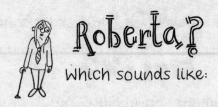

Which sounds like:

A) A boy's name
(if you take the 'a' off the end)

B) Can be shortened to:
'Rob'
(another boy's name)

'Bert'
(an old boy's name)

'Bobby'
(boy dog's name)

'Bertie' . . .

. . . need I go on??

So, everyone calls me Jelly, and when Miss Haddock got to me it got a bit complicated.

 Name? Jelly Rowntree.

 Jenny? No, **Jelly**.

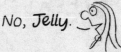 Jennifer then, no shortenings at school.

 My real name's Roberta. ←(Blank look)

 But everyone calls me Jelly. J-E-L-L-Y.
I see.

 Jellifer? What an unusual name!

But . . .

 One more peep out of you and it's twice round the playing field!

17

There was a lot of **tittering** from the rest of the class and I went **VERY RED**. Myf and Roobs were trying hard to be loyal by going red too, but I could tell they were trying even harder not to **titter**.

-3-
Big Girls

We are *EXHAUSTED!* Big School is **REALLY** stressful and <u>COMPLETELY</u> different to primary school . . .

It's gone from this

to this

$$4 \div 208.9^2 \times \frac{78.01}{1.002} =$$

in one fell swoop.

PRIMARY 98 kids

1 nice teacher all year round

(Mrs Bellatra)

All of us in 1 lovely gang

Fun games every playtime

Fun work, lots of colouring in

Wear what we like and no one cares

Great outfit, Jelly.

BIG 1,310 kids

Loads of different teachers every day

(Called 'Sir' or 'Miss')

Lots of separate gangs

Cool

Loner

Geeks

Weirdos

Bullies

Sporty

Shuffling about, pushing each other and being mean every breaktime

Hard work

He, he.

Oi, shrimp features!

$$4 \div 208.9^2 \times \frac{78.01}{1.002} =$$

no marks for colouring in

All wearing same thing but still getting bullied for what we're wearing

Check out the tie.

At the end of our first week we had a secret meeting of the Faithful Club to discuss everything that had happened.

We had just voted on whether or not we should try to become cool girls (1 yay (me) 2 nays (Myf and Roobs)) when my older brother Jay barged into my room with his guitar ...

(squeaky voice)

We are the Faithful Club . . . La, la, laaa! We la, la, la, oOOOoh . . . Can I joiny woiny?

Shuddup, Jay!

Haa, haa!

Hee, heee heee!

Ooh (giggle) I love Buster Bauble from O.M.G.!

BUSTER.

Myf and Roobs go into 'hysterics' when Jay's around. I don't find him in the **slightest** bit amusing, **especially** when his friends Brendan, Jock and Roger are around, which they virtually always are. Then he says, 'Stop showing off, Jelly!' whatever I'm doing ...

e.g.

Nothing.

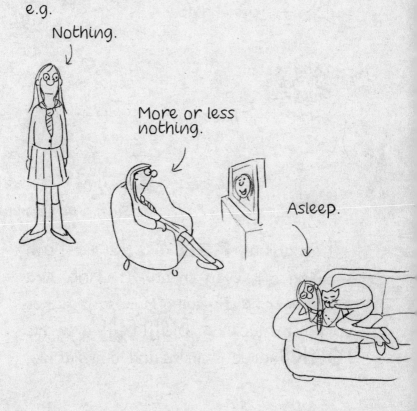

More or less nothing.

Asleep.

This is a typical exchange between me and Jay.

I always go **red** and feel like I **am** showing off, even though I'm **not**. And also Roger Lovely, who Mum says makes up for his lack of **Brain cells** with his **looks**, always smiles and winks at me.

Jay reckons himself as a songwriter and he makes up stupid songs to annoy me,

And there was Rubi
ooh-I-ee-oh-ah!
And there was Myf
ooh-I-ee-oh-ah!
And there was Ricky
ooh-I-ee-oh-ah!
And the Boss, that was Jelleee
Hi-ee-oh-hi-ee-oh-ha!

but I did manage to pick up a bit of useful info from him — **Roger Lovely** plays the guitar in the school orchestra (he's better than Jay — ha, ha, ha, ha, ha!).

-4-
Musical Statues

Myfanwy, Rubi and I are in the school orchestra! I'm not sure how cool that is, but it clashes with double games, and we are fed up with Miss Haddock making us play sport in **severe** weather conditions . . .

Blizzards   Floods   Hurricanes   Draughts

(. . . and also now I knew that Roger Lovely played guitar, it would be a chance to be near him without Jay humiliating me).

I got the triangle, Rubi got the maracas and Myf just about got the tambourine. Even though she only had to hit it once, she got an :itch: on her nose and missed the moment. No one else auditioned so Mr Bucket let her have it, on a trial basis.

We found we hardly ever had to play our instruments — so we'd get distracted, STARING at everybody else ◉ ◉ and giggling JUST as Mr Bucket would point ☞ at us to play a note. ♪

That keyboardist looks like a miniature Buster Bauble — you know, the one you **say** I fancy in O.M.G.

That's Sandy Blatch.

Who?

Sandy Blatch is very small ⅄ (he wasn't sitting down at the keyboard, but standing on a box) and as I'm now 5ft 5ins and big boned, however much he looks like Buster Bauble from O.M.G., I could **NEVER** go out with him. (**NOT** that I **a)** fancy B.B. or **b)** want to go out with anyone.)

Then :SUDDENLY: and most unusually I had a triangle **SOLO**.

While I was busy concentrating, **MYFANWY** – who is a **TERRIBLE** gossip and had only heard the words 'I', 'fancy', 'Sandy' and 'looks like Buster Bauble' – told the **WHOLE** orchestra that I fancied Sandy Blatch because I thought he looked like Buster Bauble (who we **ALL** fancy, but don't admit to it).

After one rehearsal Sandy's friend, Benji Butler, who plays the cello, said to me ...

Sandy wants to know if you like him for himself, or because he looks like Buster Bauble?

She must like him for himself!

Well, he <u>doesn't</u> look like Buster!

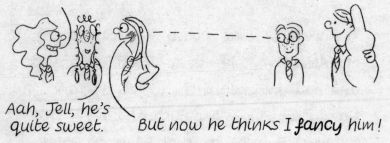

Aah, Jell, he's quite sweet.

But now he thinks I *fancy* him!

And because Sandy and Roger sit next to
↳ each other ↴

Hey, Sandy.

Hi, Roger.

How's your dad?

I couldn't even stare ◯◯ at Roger without Sandy thinking I was staring at him . . .

and I kept :binging: my triangle by
mistake. Sandy staring was making me a
NERVOUS wreck.

Mr Bucket said to me afterwards –

Your heart ♡ doesn't
seem to be in it, Jelly!
I need PASSION ! !

Can you play the
triangle with passion,
Mr Bucket?

Of course, Jelly!

We have a new girl in the school, Angel Farraday, and she's going to replace you! If you want to see the triangle played with

PASSION he SPAT

come to the school concert!

After I had wiped Mr Bucket's spit out of my eye, there was Sandy.

Don't cry, Jelly. I think you play the triangle beautifully.

I'm **not** crying.

Now I would have to go back to games with Miss  Haddock, and **WITHOUT** Myf and Roobs, but at least I wouldn't have to put up with S.B. staring at me any more . . . I **thought**.

But **NOW**, instead, wherever I went he kept popping up ₀₀₀

Boing!

Aagh!

I just couldn't shake him off!

Would you like me to carry your triangle, Jelly?

Would you like some tea, Jelly? Strong and sweet . . . like you.

Allow me, Ms Rowntree.

J-E,
J-E-L,
J-E-L-L,
JELLY!

-5-
We All Get Knits

A few weeks ago Mum gave up smoking and took up knitting instead. The first thing she knitted was a 'jumper' for her boyfriend Julian.

It was ginorMOUS

I've got an addictive personality!
I couldn't **STOP**!

At least it's not **BAD** for my **HEALTH**!

BUT it turned out it was QUITE BAD for Julian's health . . . .

IT's **AMAZING** what a dangerous weapon a knitting needle can be when handled correctly.

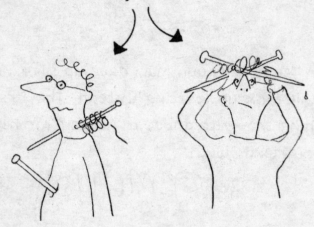

Mum went mad because Julian refused to wear the 'jumper' she'd knitted him. He *SAID* he was allergic to man-made materials like acrylic.

(REALLY he was allergic to looking like a very ugly winter bride.)

The corner shop?
Do I have to,
Susan?

Those teenagers
might be
loitering.

Just **go** –
you look
very nice!

It wasn't just Julian who didn't want to
go out for fear of ridicule – by the end
of the week Mum had kitted us all out in

Woolly outfits ....

Dog tank top

Tulip skirt

Fish scarf

Trunks and flippers

Mouse socks

Hamster muff

Julian's willy warmer

Cat poncho (matching earmuffs)

Guinea-pig frock

. . . and got very hurt if we didn't wear them.

$\mathcal{S}$O we were all very relieved when Mum said, 'I'm addicted to the gym!'

However, Julian got quite upset when Mum kept mentioning a person called giuseppe.

Shall I pick you up from the gym, Soo3?

No it's OK. giuseppe and I are jogging back together!

giuseppe says this, giuseppe says that, giuseppe says I've got very good thighs, and I'm **very** flexible, **very** firm . . .

Maybe you should knit him a **scarf** and I could **gag** him with it?

What?

39

-6-
Stalkers

Poor old Julian took to staring out of the window waiting for Mum to come home from the gym. One night I heard Cat (yes, our cat is called 'Cat') fighting outside and Julian and I banged heads trying to look out at the same time.

Ow! **Urgh!**

After swearing violently at each other the way banging heads makes you want to, we looked down to see Mum and *giuseppe* chatting at the gate, and Sandy serenading me from the pavement ₒₒₒ

Who's that little chap pretending to be Cat?

Who's that hairy man with Mum?

Sandy Blatch is very good on the keyboards but his singing was quite SCARY

♫ I just can't get you out of my brain . . . (I think that's what he was ~~miaowing~~ singing anyway.)

Mwonderful voice . . .

I explained to Julian that he was called Sandy, and he was STALKING ⚡⚡⚡⚡ me ⊙ ⊙. It didn't matter how much I 🐙 IGNORED him, or was MEAN 😠, he just wouldn't GIVE UP.

I know how he feels . . . but you know, Jells, one day he will give up and then your MU— I mean you — might be sorry.

I knew he was talking about him and Mum, as well as me and Sandy (not that there was a me and Sandy) so I offered him some advice . . . Even though Julian was quite annoying I didn't want him to leave because then Mum would start criticising me again instead.

'Maybe you should be more **mean**, Julian?'

 Why would I do that, Jells? I love your mum, so why would I be mean? It's up to her to change . . . before it's too late . . .

This sounded *quite* OMINOUS.

I tried to think of ways to **STOP** Mum going to the gym.

Mum? Will you knit me a bedspread?

Jell! You know I've given up knitting. Old lady's hobby, giuseppe says . . .

Would you like me to go out and get you some fags?

Jelly! I'd rather lick the gutter! giuseppe says . . .

It was no good. I'd have to find a NEW Addiction for Mum — Aha! I suddenly had an excellent plan!

I remembered something she was **VERY** addicted to . . . PARTIES!

Pass the Party

Mum has always been addicted to parties and as soon as Julian moved in with us 9 months ago (after Mum had nagged him incessantly to give up his bedsit in Little Boxford), she started saying,

Let's have a party!

And Julian would say,

But they'll mess the place up, Fatty will escape . . .

and what about the cream carpet?!

Mum and Julian are like CHALK  (a bit screechy) and CHEESE (a bit smelly) (of patchouli).

Mum says Julian makes her feel **SAFE**.

and Julian says Mum makes him feel **ALIVE**.

Woooo!

Mum also says Julian makes her feel **DEAD**.

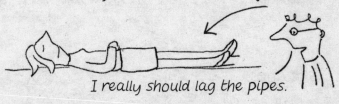

I really should lag the pipes.

and Julian says Mum makes him fear for his **LIFE**.

What do you MEAN, it looks no different? It cost £60!

Julian is _slightly_ NERVOUS of me,
my brother Jay and our seven pets (as
well as Mum) because he's never lived
with lots of people before (only Anthea).
So a few weeks ago, knowing that my
birthday was coming up, Mum tried a new
wheeze to **embarrass** Julian into
agreeing to a party.

Julian! Jelly
wants to have
a PARTY!

No, I don't.

She does.

Well, if she
really wants
one . . . .

I don't.

She does.

Well if
she . . .

I did want
one . . .

I DON'T!

. . . just give us some warning.

I DON'T WANT A PARTY !

Adults are such terrible listeners . . .

Probably all
the wine.

My mum's trying to make me have a party.

You lucky thing!

Ooh!

I only know you two and Ricky.

You could invite all the popular people.

Hmm.

They wouldn't come to my party.

Why not?

Well . . .

Well, you . . . **we're** a bit silly and childish, aren't we?

You might be.

Speak for yourself.

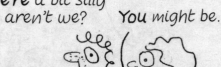

Oh, **please** have a party, Jell! Pleeeaaase! We can play Pass the Parcel and Musical Chairs . . .

Nothing dangerous.

I'm **NOT** having a **PARTY!**

Oh.

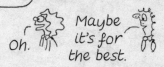

Maybe it's for the best.

I mean, someone might spill something on the carpet . . . like Caustic acid . . . and it might make a hole in the carpet and the floor, and you might fall down the hole and **DIE** and be eaten by **RATS.**

That's right, Roobs.

I told her. And Myfanwy said,

Can we have some more hot chocolate?

Then we played **FLATMATES** with our Barbie dolls (don't tell anyone).

49

But now I decided that a party was just what Mum needed to distract her from *Giuseppe* and that I would sacrifice my own feelings for the sake of Mum and Julian staying together and agree to have a party.

Mum? Can I have a birthday party?

Of course! Yes! You said you didn't want one! Julian will be thrilled! Now how long till your birthday? Only three weeks! We'd better get cracking.

–8–

Shut Up, Julian

The next night I heard Mum get home early from the gym. Julian was still in the bath. But when I looked out of the window she wasn't with *Giuseppe*, she was chatting to Sandy!

I could only hear snippets . . .

'. . . how's your mum since your . . . Aaah . . . Poor love OK, Sandy love, night, night . . . give your mum . . . Bye . . .'

WHO were you talking to outside? Julian said, looking as scary as you can in a wee willy winky night gown* and a towelling turban.

* made of natural fibre

51

Sandy Blatch, actually, a very nice friend of Jelly's.

 He's NOT a friend of mine. I was just telling Juli—

 Well, he's ever so sweet. I asked him if he wanted to come to your party.

I CAN'T BELIEVE YOU INVITED SANDY BLATCH TO MY PARTY!

 What about giuseppe? He's not coming, is he?

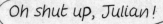 Oh shut up, Julian!

 Sorry, Sue. He's not coming though, is he?

52

While Mum started writing a party list . . .

. . . I explained my selfless ploy to Julian — that Mum would get addicted to the **PARTY** and forget about the **GYM** (*giuseppe*).

Vol-e-vents
French sticks
Play-list?
Neighbour
Garden lights
Fatty? Cat?

He looked quite pleased 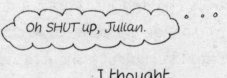 but then he looked worried and said, 'What about the cream carpet?'

Oh SHUT up, Julian.

I thought.

I only had **three weeks** until the party and at the moment I only had **three people** to invite. **WHY** had I suggested it? It's embarrassing enough being me without celebrating it with a party . . .

But then something **UNBELIEVABLE** happened to take my mind off it . . . .

53

-9-
Personal Remarks

Even though I am the third worst at games in the whole school I have just WON ① the

CROSS COUNTRY!

It all started when I was walking across the playground towards the gym for double games (having just eaten a double portion of sponge pudding and custard) and Miss Haddock shouted ...

Jellifer Rowntree!
Your bottom is
S-P-R-E-A-D-I-N-G!
More runs,
less buns!!

snigger

Apart from the embarrassment of having my jodhpur thighs mentioned in a **LOUD VOICE**, she still insisted on calling me 'Jellifer' – usually causing some passer-by to snigger.

Anyway, **TODAY** she gathered us all together and sprang the cross country on us with an evil glint in her eye. She said,

'You'll all be pleased to know (long pause, like on **X** THE FACTOR) that today is the . . . . cross country! Get your kit on and line up against the wall in the playground.' ('And I will machine-gun you all to death,' she may as well have added.)

Her announcement was met by **149 girls** groaning and Cicily Fanshaw shrieking, '**YIPPEE!**' She won all the running races at primary school by miles.

But, Miss . . . !

I began.

(Deep breath)

1, 2, 3, 4, 5, 6, 7, 8, 9, 10,

Yes, Jellifer?

'I haven't got my kit, Miss!' I wailed.

'Spare kit in the box!' she yelled.

Cringing, I put on someone else's stinky top and someone else's stinky shorts.

POO!

Aha! There were **NO** stinky trainers in the stinky box!

I hurried to Miss Haddock, trying
not to let any of the stinky
outfit touch my skin.

'Miss!! No trainers!'

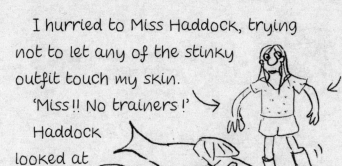

Haddock
looked at
my feet.

'You'll have to run in those.'

'But, Miss! I ca-a-a-a-an't!!' I wailed.

I was wearing Julian's size **11** wellies
because it was **raining** and Mum made me
walk to school and I forgot my shoes.

So I tried a few other ploys on Haddock:

Jellifer Rowntree!
Straighten up!

I can't, Miss! I've got a stitch!

Well you shouldn't
eat so much!

I've got my period!

Exercise is good for cramps.

I've gone blind!

It's good for your eyes.

Who am I?

It's especially good for your memory.

I was walking at the back of the trotting crowd of girls with Karen Ryan (who is already engaged) and Cheryl Gluck 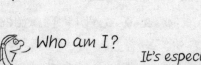 (who already works in her mum's hairdressers).

We were even overtaken by Bethany Iceland and the 'Popular girls', who, though they had the latest fashion sports gear, were far too cool to run. I'm sure I heard one of them say 'spreading Bottom,' but then Bethany said,

Hi, Jelly, how are you?

Bethany and I used to play together when we were 4.

And even though she was now a cool girl, she wasn't completely **COLD** – she still said hello to me.

Then they all started doing girly giggling and I realised we were about to pass the BOYS playing football, and *leaning* on the railings THERE was Roger Lovely.

Roger has been kept back two years but looks about 17. My mum says he's SWEET-but-THICK but I think he's 'Lovely' – and about to look round and see me in my stinky outfit and GIANT wellies!

I couldn't decide whether to . . .

cross my arms to cover my minuscule bosoms

OR

put my hands over my spreading bottom.

Instead I tried to run backwards through
the puddles with my arms folded – but my
wellies were so full of water I could hardly
lift them! So I shuffled behind a tree and
decided to wait there
until Roger had gone.

I didn't think he'd
seen me . . . but
Sandy Blatch
had.
GOOD!!

Surely he will go off me **now**? I thought.
I even stuck my welly
out so he could have
a good look . . .

–10–

Personal Remarks
Part Two

I was quite happy to wait there until **Roger** had gone – I didn't care if I came completely and totally last in the cross country. But **THEN** Karen Ryan and Cheryl Gluck – the only threats to my position as utterly ~~LAST~~ appeared behind my tree ...

... and tried to **SQUASH** in.

But bits of
them were ST*i*_c_K*i*ng
out.

When I told them Your bits are
sticking out.

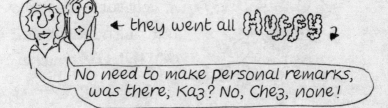 ← they went all **HUFFY**

No need to make personal remarks,
was there, Kaz? No, Chez, none!

'But what are you DOING?' I asked them.

'Miss Haddock's out there! She'll make
us **run**!' they wailed.

'My heels are killin' me,' Karen said.

'Yeah, an' me,' Cheryl agreed.

I peeped round the tree. →

Oh no! – **Rōger Lŏvely** was still there
. . . But so was Miss 🐟 🦐 AND she was
👄 TALKING to **him**! 👤

THEN the worst thing that could possibly
happen, happened.

Our dog, Fatty, appeared in the trees
C O V E R E D in vegetable peelings
and with a WHOLE
𝕸𝕺𝖀𝕷𝕯𝖄 chicken
in his mouth.

He'd obviously escaped again and
done his usual routine, a trip to the bins
🗑️ round the back 🗑️ of the shops 🏢 →

on his way to see his girlfriend 🐕
in Lower Boxford.

This was obviously his route **EVEN**
though dogs weren't allowed on the
playing field.

64

Then I heard Haddock's shrieky voice –
'There's a dog in the poplars! You, boy!
Get him!'

screeched Karen and Cheryl.

'Pleeeeaaaase don't let it be **ROGER**!'
I prayed – out loud obviously, because
Karen said, 'Who? Oh, **ROGER** Luvlee! Yeah,
cor, if I wasen' engaged I'd go for 'im.'

'Yeh. Bit fick though . . .' Cheryl added.

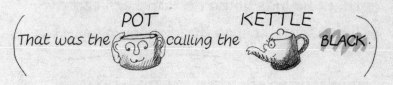

That was the POT calling the KETTLE BLACK.

'Certainly, Miss Haddock,' said **ROGER**
in his lovely deep lovely voice that was
getting CLOSER and CLOSER.

Fatty spotted me at that point, dropped his mouldy chicken and started jumping up and down . . .

No need to make personal remarks, Jelly!

Go away, Fatty!

'I'm **talking** to the dog,' I told them.

Though Fatty was on a walk already, the sound of any word that sounded like w-a-l-k – like t-a-l-k(ing) made him think he was going on another (better?) walk so he jumped up and down even . . .

Fetch, boy!

. . . higher

OI! -FATTY!

'Go on, boy! You can catch him! Fetch!'
Haddock shouted to ROGER as if HE
were a dog . . . There was nothing for it —
I would have to actually RUN !

But when I attempted to break
into a run Cheryl and Karen
became hysterical, staggering
after me and clawing at my Aertex
shirt, clumps of mud attaching themselves
to their high heels.

But THEN ahead of us ———▷ an
even WORSE thing than fatso turning
up — MUM! Heading from the super-
market car park looking like a RAGING
BULL !

FATTY!
Come
here!

Cooee!
Fatty
dear!

Shut UP,
Julian!

It's quite difficult to climb a tree in wellies but I had no choice – Mum and Julian were coming one way – Fatty, Roger Lovely and Haddock were coming the other – I was out of sight but Karen and Cheryl hid behind it with all their bits sticking out again.

It was quite funny watching Mum being told off by Miss Haddock.

Is this your dog, Mrs Rowntree?

Not exactly.

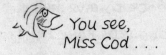 You see,
Miss Cod . . .  Haddock

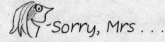 Sorry, Mrs . . .  Miss

Sorry! You see, Miss Haddock, he **was** our dog but we lost touch . . .

How **are** things?

GRRR . . .

See! Never got on!

I see.

Anyway — titter —
we're lost basically —
we came out of TeSCO's
car park and . . .

I waited for Miss Haddock to give her a detention or at least two laps round the field, **BUT**...

'Hmph,' she said. 'Well, I better get off and patrol the cross country. Get rid of the dog,' she told **Roger**, while she stomped back to her hatchback.

Julian pretended to do up his shoelaces...

... and Mum over-thanked **Roger** (who looked quite confused). They were **HANGING ABOUT** so they could claim ownership of Fatty without Haddock seeing.

As soon as she  **SCREECHED** off,

they took Fatty from **Roger**
and dragged him away ...

Now, Chez, Kaz (as I had come to know
them) and I (Jez) really <u>WERE</u> lost. So we
trudged through the trees till we came
to a road. Trying to get our bearings,
we turned a corner and heard Haddock
shouting,

Come on, girls, keep
going – you're in
the lead – RUN !!!

I had a pint of water in each welly and
Kaz and Chez still clinging to me, **BUT**
Cicily Fanshaw was coming up behind us,

doing that smug upright running, bunches
swinging and not 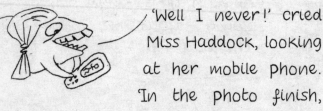 Out the way,
fatties!
a bead of sweat
on her.

Oi!

I had only a few <u>F e e t</u> to go
so I forced myself to sprint, pushing my
SIZE **11** welly across the line — Kaz and
Chez, so used to me being their leader,
pushed themselves forward too.

'Well I never!' cried
Miss Haddock, looking
at her mobile phone.
'In the photo finish,
Jellifer has just pipped Cicily at the post!'

I've never won nuffin' in my life.

Not at all put off.

Miss! Jelly must've cheated. I was in the lead the whole way!

Don't be such a BAD SPORT, Cicily! No one cheated. I would have seen them.

I'M NOT A BAD SPORT, Miss!

Cicily yelled and got a detention for answering back, *Whereas* Kaz, Chez and I got a lift to school in Miss Haddock's hatchback.

-11-
Misrepresenting the School

The next morning, I was walking to the bus stop, and there, annoyingly, was Sandy Blatch. **ALSO THERE**, not _at all_ annoyingly, was Röger Lövely.

Ignoring Sandy, I said, 'Hello, Röger!' and got ready to tell him about my triumph in the cross country ① but he had his headphones 🎧 on . . .

Sandy said, 'Good morning, my Jellivescent!'

'Is your name Röger?' I said coldly.

'No. It's Sandy,' he replied, all innocent. Then he opened his blazer . . .

. . . just as the bus arrived.

The bus driver said,

We used to call that
-FLASHING-
in my day, love.

And the whole bus LAUGHED hur, hur, hur.

   There were only two seats on the bus —
one next to a woman with no teeth,
drinking beer and shouting swear words,
and one next to Sandy,

**** OFF,
YOU ****!

I'm only sitting next to
you because I don't want
to sit next to her.

I understand, Jelly.
I'm quite chuffed
you prefer me.

It was just then that **Röger L** decided
to spot me.

Hi, JELLS!

he shouted
to the
whole bus.

Hi, Sandy! Like your T-shirt.
Ah, sweet! Are you two an item?
You make a nice COUPLE!

(As he loped off I could tell he was **very**
disappointed, but he covered it up well.)

Look, Sandy, I don't want to be
mean but I can't hang around with
you. It's not **PERSONAL**.

Oh, Jelly! You're so fiery and strong . . .
and your hair is like GOLDEN SILK . . .

Really?

Oh, what was
the **point**?

I rushed off as soon as the bus stopped – my hair flowing like golden silk. I didn't want to be late, because it was ⸬FRIDAY⸬ and I didn't want to miss a second of my FAVOURITE lesson: BIOL☺GY. It's SO exciting . . .

I've sucked a SLUG into a teat pipette!!!
I've sucked a SLUG into a TEAT PIPETTE!!!

Our biology teacher, Miss Jasmine, is my favourite teacher. BUT unfortunately I am NOT her favourite pupil.

Jelly Rowntree! WHY is it always YOUR voice I can hear above everyone else's?!

And she always sends me outside - all for being ~`ENTHUSIASTIC`~.

I HATE Miss Jasmine.

me too.

While standing outside the classroom AGAIN due to my *fasCINation* with my favourite subject, along lolloped Miss Haddock . . .

Ah! Jellifer! Just the young lady I wanted to see!! Now, the cross country championships are two weeks on Saturday – of course with your time of 4.48 minutes you will be representing the school.

'But, Miss, I cheated, I **told** you!' I whined.

'Nonsense, Jellifer. I saw you **WIN** the cross country with my own eyes!'

'But . . .' I whimpered.

'Oh, stop being modest – wearing wellies isn't **cheating**! I'll pick you up from your mother's. And make sure you wear your lucky wellies again.'

'But, Miss Haddock, I **ran** through the wood – not even **RAN** – walked! Miss **Haddock**!' I yelled after her.

Just then Miss Jasmine threw open the classroom door and shouted, 'Jelly! Be quiet! Don't you **ever** shut up?!'

Then she noticed Miss Haddock . . .

'Oh, h-h-h-hello, Miss H-H-Haddock.'

All the teachers were scared of Miss

Haddock because of her **FORCEFUL** personality and her constant attempts to start a teacher's hockey team. Miss Jasmine **blushed** and **retreated**. I noticed that she had developed a LIMP.

The kind that would make it **VERY** difficult to play hockey . . .

Self-hypnosis

Standing outside the classroom humming to myself, I started to believe I really **HAD** won the cross country.

It was the photographic proof,

my fake gold medal,

the applause,

the way **Roger Lovely** said,  I like sporty girls.

and Miss Haddock seeing it with her very own eyes!

I became self-hypnotised by all the evidence.

I HAD WON THE CROSS COUNTRY!

Just then Bethany Iceland and the cool girls went by.

Hi, Jelly. How are you?

Why couldn't I have friends like that? I thought.

But winning the cross country had **boosted** my feelings of self-worth and Myfanwy and Rubi were squashing their faces against the window in a most **immature** way, so I took my chance –

Um, Bethany? Would you like to come to my party a week on Saturday? Bring anyone you like. Like everyone you know?

Yeah sure, Jells. I've got a few parties that night, but I'll try and pop in.

I was so pleased with myself for doing something so SCARY that I didn't even care that they laughed as they walked off.

Ha, ha, ha, ha, ha ha, ha, ha, ha ha ha, ha, ha . . .

-13-

party Rules

Often I can't sleep for **worrying** but then I wake up 👀 and realise I've got no reason to be worried!

BUT since I'd invited Bethany to my party, and Mum had asked **Roger Lovely** to come and keep an eye on the pets, I'd wake up and realise I had **EVERY REASON** to be worried!

I kept seeing the party through THEIR eyes.

And it wasn't a pretty sight.

I decided to tell Mum I wanted to cancel it . . . but the trouble was, she just wouldn't understand. She's always had a bit of trouble understanding me.

Like when I was **SIX** ∘∘∘∘∘∘∘∘∘∘∘∘

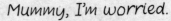

Mummy, I'm worried.

What about?

Well . . . what **are** we?

We're people, silly moo.

Yes, but what **are** people?

Where does the sky end? And where were we before we were born?

Wha'?

Oh, it doesn't matter, Mummy.

How about we go up town tomorrow and get you a nice frock . . .

86

. . . *that'll take your mind off things.*

OK, Mummy.

Mum's nice but she never seems to wonder about anything. Like the weirdness of being ⁓alive⁓ in a **GIANT** universe or what makes Fatty suddenly decide to get up and leave the room for no apparent reason.

She likes clothes, 👕 and 🗣 gossip and parties. 🥂

She's not the sort of person who would lie awake at night worrying and imagining all sorts of terrible things.

So when I woke her up at 3.40 a.m., I didn't elaborate.

I don't want to have a party.

Oh, **pleeeease**, Jell, I'm so looking forward to it.

That's partly what I'm worried about.

In the end Mum promised to:

Only be around for the first two hours, then go and watch telly in her room.

Have Fatty sedated so he would sleep through the whole thing upstairs.

Encourage (**force**) Julian to take up an offer to teach an aromatherapy weekend.

Lavender — for stress or if you have trouble sleeping . . .

. . . and Ricky Chin promised not to do his party trick,

Urgh! Urgh! Urgh!

drinking Coke through his nose and then break-dancing whilst burping the *Match of the Day* theme (quite impressive actually).

And I made Mum promise to buy me a **JUMPER** for my birthday that I had seen at the shopping centre – black and **FLUFFY** with a hood (Bethany Iceland had one). I told her **EXACTLY** which one, and how much, and where, so she couldn't get it **WRONG**.

-14-

Horse Poo

But now was the difficult bit — getting Rubi and Myfanwy not to be immature and a silly.

I imagined myself as one of the cool girls:

somehow being a cool girl would make me lose weight, have thick silky hair and own an iPhone.

Of course, I would still say hello to Myf and Roobs.

Oh, hi, you two.

Hi, Jelly.

Jelly!

They were coming round later, I would
subtly mention it to them then . . .

LATER ...

Hi, Jellywelly! We're herey-werey for the
Faithfully-Waithfully Clubby-
Wubby meety-weeting!

For goodness sake! If you don't stop
being so silly and childish you're not
allowed to come to my party-warty . . . .

ahem . . —PARTY.

We're not silly
and childish.
We're
NOT, NOT,
NOT!

'Oh look,' I told them in a **cold** voice. 'Maybe we should close the club down. I mean we're a bit **OLD** for it now.'

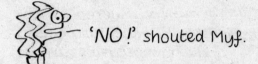 'NO!' shouted Myf.

'Well,' said Roobs. 'We might regret closing it down.'

We don't want to close it down! Won't! Won't! Won't! We're faithful till we die like we promised and you're breaking your promise!

'Oh **all right**,' I told them. 'But I've decided I want a *Grown-Up* party — talking and music, no games or cake . . .'

No games?

No cake
or jelly?

And there might be
boys . . . not just Ricky.

Boys?

Yuck!

I think we should mix
around a bit, get some
more friends . . .

What friends?

We don't
want more
friends!

I tried to be **hard** but there was something pathetic about them.

squeak

squeak

So let's be a bit more mature at the party, OK?

What does 'mature' **mean**, anyway?

Sort of . . . **old**.

OK, Jelly, we can be manure.

Mature.

Hur hurr hurr! **Manure** hur hurr . . .

A-ha-ha-ha-eee that's hor-ho-ho-horse POO-oo-ee ha-ha-ha!

Roger Napoleon

Myf and Roobs were round for tea and Myf had done her history homework in record time.

	1) WHICH COUNTRY WAS NAPOLEON EMPEROR OF?
	Rome! (Durr!)
O	**2) WHAT COUNTRIES DID HE CONQUER?**
	Essicks, Kent, Suffolk (of course)
	3) WHERE WAS THE BATTLE OF WATERLOO FOUGHT?
O	Waterloo Station (obviousleeee!)
	4) WHERE DID NAPOLEON LIVE HIS LAST DAYS?
	Old people's home (dumbo)

Shh . . . I'm trying to get them right.

Done it! Hurry up!

So am I.

Maybe we should get some **kissing** practice in before your party.

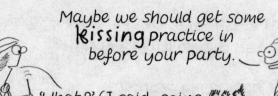

'What?' (I said, going *red* – I'd already been practising).

I **know**.

Not with each other!

'It's just that, you know, there's going to be boys there. We might play kiss chase!' she said, not going red.

What about germs?

I've told you – **no** games. Just chatting, dancing, eating.

And **kissing**?

Mwah! Mwah . . .

I don't know! Who are **you** planning to **kiss**?

Is your brother going to be there? I'd like to **kiss** him!

Even though Myf is the MOST embarrassing she is also the least ~embarrassed~.

You're hoping my brother is going to kiss **YOU**! He's far too **OLD**, far too **TALL** and he's a complete **DRONGO**.

Still not going red.

So? ———

What's a drongo? ———

The height difference between Myf and Jay was even bigger than it was between me and Sandy . . .

TESCO

'Look, Myf, he only likes older girls
(even though he's a giant baby)
and anyway he's got a girlfriend.'
(His latest, Carla 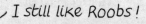, was quite nice –
she wouldn't last.)

So ? I don't care !

Just because you don't
like me and Roobs any more . . .

Not that I care !

'That's not true', I said, trying for a jokey
tone.

I still like Roobs !

Why don't you like
Myf any more ?

Shuddup, Jelly ! I hate you !

Myf looked so crestfallen I decided to show her my kissing-practice partner to cheer her up.

It was my grandmother's old bust of Napoleon (I ignored Myf sniggering at the word 'BUST').

He was a bit cold and stiff but then so were a lot of men, my mum said.

Careful,

You don't know where he's been.

Who are you pretending it is? Sandy Blatch?

No !!!

Yes you are! Yes you are!

I was so outraged, I told her . . .

Actually, Roger Lovely.

 Roger Lovely?!
Your brother's
friend? But how
come **HE'S** not too **mature** for YOU?

Is it because he's so **THICK**
he's been held back two years?

 NO, it's
because I'm
more mature
than YOU.

NOT
NOT
NOT
AM

AM
AM
AM
NOT

 Ha, ha, ha, ha, ha!
YOU said **NOT**!

'SHUDDUP, MYF,' I told her.

Then, just as I puckered up
to kiss **Roger**. . .

Mmmm, **Roger**. . .

–16–
Slave Trade

. . . Jay burst in.

Mum said you've got to take Fatt— Roger? Roger who?

Hello, Jay!
(titter)
He-he-hello, Jay.

Get out!

What are you two up to . . . ?

We're practising our kissing! Jelly's practising to kiss Roger Lovely.

Shh!

'Oh yes?' my brother said, doing his dead-eyed ⊙ ⊙ smile at me, the one he does when he's trying to get his **one** brain cell to work. It's similar to the one I do when I'm trying to pee in the sea. →

'Aha! So **that's** why you were so keen for him to come on Saturday, **NOT** because he's good with animals.' →

To distract him I started saying,

And Myfanwy is practising to kiss . . .

(Finally going red)

At this point Myf had a massive fit of immaturity and started . . .

screaming,   singing,   flinging herself about . . .

Aaah!

La, la, la, laaah!

. . . and putting her hands over my mouth.

M-m-m-m.

She's gone mad. Should we call an ambulance?

ROW! ROW! ROW!

But my brother didn't seem interested in who Myf was practising to **kiss** . . . He just **winked** at me and said, 'Don't worry Jells. I'll take Fatty out, maybe I'll walk around to **Roger**'s.'

Ooh er, he's going to tell Roger, Jelly.

'You've done it now!' I said to Myfanwy.

Done wha'?

D'you think I seemed a
bit immature or did I get
away with it?

Two days passed and I was in a state of
heightened TENSION — was my brother
going to tell Roger?

. . . Until **one** evening he said,

If you pick the
dandruff out
of my hair I'll
give you 50p.

£1

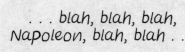

But then someone
on the telly said,

. . . blah, blah, blah,
Napoleon, blah, blah . . .

105

And some small memory flickered across his brain cell (making his dandruff dr̊p like a $nowstorm. URGH!)

'Do it for nothing or I'll tell R☺ger you fancy him,' he said.

'I don't fancy him!'

'Oh well. You won't mind if I tell him about your **Kissing** practice – where's his number . . .? Oh no, it's OK, he's coming over in a bit . . .'

Pleeeeeeasee don't tell him! NOT that I do!

He said if I agreed to be his slave for a month he wouldn't tell R☺ger.

I'd been his slave before so I knew what it entailed:

1. Tea delivered at 7.40 a.m., three sugars
2. Making plates of sweet and savoury snacks on demand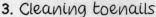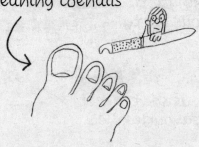
3. Cleaning toenails

4. Removing unsightly items (mouldy cups/clumps of sticky fluff) from under his bed
5. Feeding, walking, cleaning out all the pets (including his locusts)

Hurro Jerry

6. Ironing his shirts, ties, socks, under-pants, £5 notes, homework, etc.
7. Giving him sole charge of the remote control
8. Calling him 'Your Highness'

. . . and general assistance whenever requested.

When **Roger** arrived he was his usual
kind and wonderful self . . .

Hello, Jell, how are you?
I'm looking forward to
your party.

I . . .

She's fine, Jay.

Get us some sweet
'n' savouries, Jells.

Yes, Your Highness.

From the kitchen I heard,

'AW, your little sister's so sweet.'

Sweet? I'd heard Mum saying
Julian was sweet and **NOT**
in a very **sweet** voice.

'Only cos I told her if she wasn't sweet
I'd tell you she fancied you.'

I stood stock-still in the kitchen doorway. There was a five-second pause . . .

Jay had seen the plates of food enter the room before me, so he tried to cover up (his stomach is bigger than his brain cell).

stomach   brain cell

'Only joking, mate,' he said. 'Don't panic, she's not going to go for a lump like you.'

'What d'you mean?' ROger enquired. And when I delivered the plates of food he looked confused (lovelorn?).

17

Stink Bombs for the Mature

Myf, Roobs and I were starting to get quite EXCITED about the party now and I persuaded them to go to Boxford shopping centre and get some stuff to make us look more grown-up.

Roobs bought:

Clip-on earrings

I bought:

Myf bought:

She promised to save them till after the party (with only a *VAGUE* threat from me to tell Jay about her ~~kissing~~ practice).

Then I had the horrible realisation that the party was only a week away . . . and I had only invited **11** people.

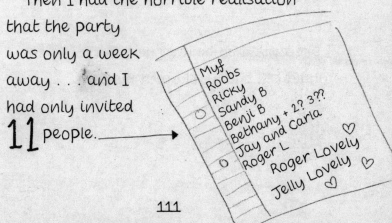

Myf
Roobs
Ricky
Sandy B
Benji B
Bethany + 2? 3??
Jay and Carla
Roger L
Roger Lovely ♡
Jelly Lovely ♡

So I said to Myf, 'Don't tell anyone I'm having a party. It's a secret.'

But Myf can't keep secrets, Jelly!

Shhh . . .

The word `secret` has a similar effect on Myf as a button that says DON'T PRESS on a **FOUR**-year-old.

OK, Jells, your secret's safe with me.

I pretended to believe her, knowing she would tell the world and his wife . . .

GUESS WHAT, DON'T TELL ANYONE BUT THERE'S A PARTY!

I told you!

(All I can say is, THANKGOD her mum didn't let her have a Facebook account.)

It was a relief when my actual birthday was over. It was on the day before the party and I managed to keep it quiet at school because Jay told me that if everyone finds out, you get pelted with eggs ○○🥚 and flour ⋰⋱. We had a small tea after school with Myf, Roobs, Ricky and Dot, and I opened my presents. There were **NO** surprises...

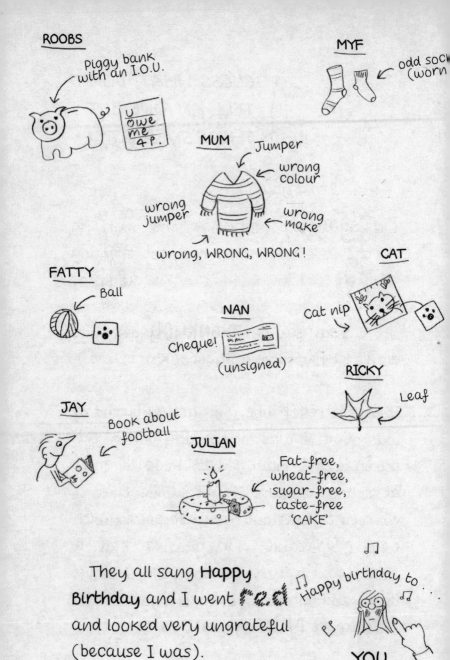

ROOBS

Piggy bank with an I.O.U.

U owe me 4p.

MYF

odd sock (worn

MUM

Jumper

wrong colour

wrong jumper

wrong make

wrong, WRONG, WRONG!

FATTY

Ball

NAN

Cheque!

(unsigned)

CAT

Cat nip

RICKY

Leaf

JAY

Book about football

JULIAN

Fat-free, wheat-free, sugar-free, taste-free 'CAKE'

They all sang **Happy Birthday** and I went **red** and looked very ungrateful (because I was).

Happy birthday to...

YOU

18

We've Been Rumbled

By Saturday morning (the morning of the PARTY!), Mum had got the dog sedated and locked him in **The Room of Doom**, Cat had been sent next door to Dot's, and Julian had grudgingly set off to his aromatherapy workshop.

Mum had been cooking all week and hadn't been to the gym **AT ALL** – so at least my **PLAN**, though *stressful*, was paying off.

Sandy Blatch and his friend Benji arrived first (twenty-five minutes early) when I'd just got in the bath. I **TRIED** not to look annoyed that he'd bought me a bunch of roses and done something **Stupid** with his *hair*

His eyes went . . .

and his hair p⚙pped back to its usual style

when he saw me wrapped in the bath mat.

(Jay and Mum had left a t-r-a-i-l
of wet towels around the house as usual.)
When I came back down (no time to do
face pack, arrange hair grip or apply
rouge – cheeks naturally **crimson**
now anyway) Benji had eaten half the

buffet and Sandy seemed to have *grown* →

several inches . . .

But when I stared at the floor to avoid
his intense gaze I noticed he was
wearing **High Heels**. _Blurgh!_ →

Roobs, Myf and Ricky arrived on the
dot of five. Rubi had shared her face pack
and **Sparkly** stuff with Myf and they
both had **rashes** and Rubi's ears
had swollen up from the clip-on earrings . . . .

Is it Halloween already, girls?

I hate being mature.

It might be terminal.

Even they weren't **silly** enough not to realise how **silly** they looked, and they huddled in the **shadows** giving me dirty looks . . .

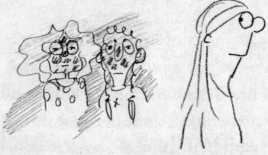

which were quite hard to ignore as they were the only ones in the room apart from Sandy, Benji, Mum and Ricky.

Then no one turned up for a **WHOLE HOUR**. It was a **VERY** tense time.

Mum got Ricky's mum and dad, and Cat, back round to fill the room up and there was polite chat and **embarrassed** silences.

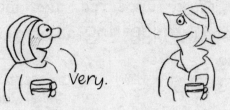

Warm for the time of year . . .

Very.

My face was still bright red from my bath and Sandy was ⊙⊙ STARING . . .

The front door bell !!!! Oh, music to my ears! Everybody, including Cat, bustled to the door . . . The **whOle** school was outside with Bethany, Jade, Kiera and Billy Rumble, the scariest boy in the school, heading them up . . .

OK, not the **wHOLE** school, but a lot of them (but not **Roger Lovely** who still hadn't arrived . . .). They all piled in.

Jay and Carla appeared and were standing about *sniggering* at everyone and saying:

> Ah, sweet, d'you remember when we were like this?

Carla told me that Sandy was wearing 'Cuban heels' and they must be his Dad's because **SHORT** people used to wear them in the **80s** to make themselves **taller** – her grandad had some.

Benji said Sandy's dad wasn't **SHORT**, he was just in a wheel-chair – he was actually **tall** – and was there any more buffet?

That was the last bit of scintillating conversation I heard before the din drowned us out. Where was Mum anyway?

The place was so :n°isy- and CROWDED
I couldn't see her — and her two hours
weren't up yet . . . I started to look for her
anxiously — I would actually be relieved
to see her in her '1980s jump suit that
still fits me!' now.

I couldn't shake Sandy
off and could hear his
Cuban heels clack-clacking
after me . . .

clack   clack

Oh my God — the living room was like
a chimps' tea-party, chimps everywhere,
you couldn't *MOVE*. I heard a Coke can
being opened — oh please,
Ricky, no, not your
party trick! There
isn't the floor
space . . .

But then a geyser of Coke
shot up and hit the white
polystyrene tiles on the ceiling . . .

–19–

Fat and Disorderly

Some of the cool girls found a bottle of Mum's cooking sherry and started passing it round and one of the cool boys put on some really :LOUD: music, the sort Mum said hadn't got any tune (and I secretly agreed).

'Great party, babe,' the cool boy said to me.

Clack, clack, clack.

D'you want me to sort them out for you? Sandy shouted up to me.

NO,

I shouted back down to him.

Where **WAS** Mum? I was getting scared now. I went upstairs to find her. She was nowhere to be seen!

I decided to look in **The Room of Doom** where Fatty had been imprisoned but I couldn't open the door. Then I saw him STAGGERING about like a drunkard on the landing trying to bark . . .

Uwrrurghooh!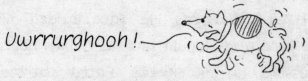

The drug had worn off!

'Fatty!' I shouted, but he teetered into Mum's bedroom.

I was lying front down on the floor peering underneath Mum's bed having just caught Fatty's gleaming, skew-wiffy eye . . .

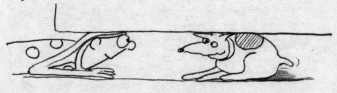

. . . when Sandy came clacking in saying 'D'you want a hand, Jells? I'm good with dog . . . Aaargh!'

His Cuban heels had come into contact with Mum's hair straighteners and he fell on top of me just as I stood up . . .

I fell backwards. His face landed on my face and I could feel his Cuban heels pressing on my knees. Fatty started b**aRKi**ng, the bedroom door _flew_ open, the light -pinged- on and Jay and Carla and a large crowd burst out laughing at the sight of me '**Kissing**' a Buster Bauble doll.

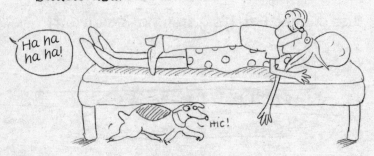

Ha ha ha ha!

Hic!

Fatty started ATTACKING Sandy's Cuban heel and managed to pull one off and stagger away with it.

He wasn't interested in biting the cool people (who were now dancing *wildly* and wrecking the place) but only in Sandy's Cuban heel.

I was trying to shout to the cool people that it was time to go home but they couldn't hear me. Then the music clicked off so suddenly that one of the cool girls was still shouting to her friend,

My thong's gone up my bum!

She obviously blamed Sandy who had his
finger on the off button  because
when he limped over and said
in quite an authoritative voice,

It's very disrespectful to Jelly's
parents — you weren't even invited.
Please can you leave now.

Who is this
little toerag
anyways?

she spat,

'Ere, wasn't you the girl who played the
piano in the Christmas concert?

joined in Billy Rumble, the scariest boy in
the school.

'Yeah, shrimp features,' continued Thong-bum, 'Wha's it got to do with you?'

'Hey, everyone! We wanna carry on partying, don't we?!' Billy yelled to the crowd. Then to me and my friends in particular,

DON'T WE?

Some people had slunk off home, but the Faithful Club was still there. (How I loved them suddenly, *rashes* and everything. I never want to leave the Faithful Club and join the cool gang.) But all of us, except Myf, were too scared to argue with Billy . . .

Y-y-yes, B-B-Billy.

So shove off, titch.

No, why should I?

There's a bit of a stink in here! Isn't there?

Y-y-yes, Billy!

I think it's a bit crowded. It would be great if somebody left.

Billy turned to me. 'Well, I think it should be *twinkletoes* here, don't you, Jelly?'

Yes. Please leave, Sandy.

Sandy gave me a terrible look.

Fine. I'm going.

I was ashamed BUT I was also
frightened of Billy like the others
were and didn't want to make a
fool of myself. And also I thought,
selfishly, at least he'll get the
message now . . .

I watched Sandy stroke Fatty's tummy,
even though he was upset, and gently
retrieve his boot.

All right, boy?

Then heard him clack, clack, clack down
the path.

All at once I felt really **BAD** for Sandy
and ran out after him . . .

Sandy! I'm sorry!

 Get back to — your party, Jelly.

Then **Roger Lovely** appeared with an injured pigeon in a box, and Jay and Carla in tow.

What's going on, Sandy, mate, you OK?

I saw Sandy's mouth moving and **Roger** nodding sympathetically.

While **Roger** shooed people out of the kitchen, I went back into the living room. Myf and Roobs had come out of the shadows. Myf (<u>NOT</u> a girl of her word) had put her whoopee cushion where Billy

131

Rumble was about to sit but Bethany sat on it just as Roobs let off a STINK BOMB...

Por! Befnee! You farted! You stink, you dirty animal!

Beff! Come on! Por! Everybody blows off, darlin'! It was those bhajis.

Bethany *stormed* out and Billy followed her, but their relationship was obviously over. (Bethany had <u>NEVER</u> farted and had only burped three times as a baby).

Then Røger spoke **FIRMLY** to the rest, who promptly filed out obediently, congratulated Myf and Roobs on their bravery,

Giss us a kiss, Røger.

and gave me a l👀K that didn't bode too well for our future together.

-20-

Man Up

Now everyone had gone and there was
LOADS of clearing up to do,
I REALLY started
to wonder where
Mum was (she was **EXCELLENT** at clearing
up) when Julian appeared, looking white
as a sheet.

'Julian! I thought you were . . . ?'

'The aromatherapy weekend was cut
short due to a . . . little disagreement,' he
sniffed.

No, Enid, I've **TOLD** you,
lavender is for **STRESS**.

sorry.

'Where's Mum?' I asked him.

'Upstairs with *giuseppe*,' he snivelled.

Then he *burst* into tears and went out into the garden to beat his chest and *hug* the tree.

sue!
suuue!

Silly old fart!

(He'd been on a Man-up weekend the week before – 'That was a waste of £200,' Mum said.)

It turned out Mum had gone in to check on Fatty, Fatty had lolloped through her legs, the ironing board had *fallen* on the door and wedged it shut . . .

. . . and she had been locked in **The Room of Doom**.

Fattay!

The Room of Doom began life as a box of doom, full of things we don't want or use.

I'm sick of this box lying about!

BOX.

Then the box went in a cupboard that became the Cupboard of Doom.

I'm sick of this cupboard! Something always falls on my head when I open it!

Not long after, **The Room of Doom** was born.

When she got locked in she tried **SHOUTING** and calling but no one heard her. So she phoned *giuseppe* on his mobile and asked him to come and rescue her.

After *giuseppe* had climbed in the window, Fatty reeled past and knocked the ladder down with Sandy's Cuban heeled boot. Then they were both trapped in **The Room of Doom**.

'Very cosy,' scowled Julian.

'But even *giuseppe* couldn't move the ironing board to open the door,' said Mum in a surprised voice.

He's not as tough as he thinks.

He's got a partially dislocated shoulder.

'Oh, that's right! Defend him!' Julian shrieked, and flounced off, slamming the door. But he got a bit of his maxi-jumper caught in the door and had to open it again _slightly_ to pull it through and click it shut again. His dramatic exit was __ruined__.

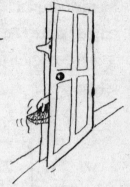

Mum laughed and Julian shouted from behind the door,

Don't laugh at me, Susan!

Oh, where's your sense of humour, Julian?!

Broken, like my heart, Susan! I'm leaving you!

Ten minutes later we saw Julian dragging a large suitcase on wheels across the lawn and he, and it, disappeared into his aromatherapy shed, and the flowery curtains that the Faithful Club had put up were whisked shut.

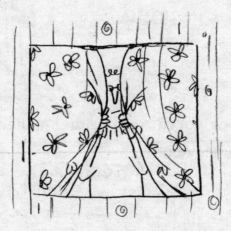

'Oh, he is a silly fart!' Mum said, laughing LOUDLY and somewhat unwisely.

'Anyway, darling,' she said, putting her arm round me (she hadn't seen the polystyrene ceiling tiles yet), 'your little friend Sandy heard us shouting and rescued us by putting the ladder up again.'

I gulped with shame (about Sandy) and fear (Mum was just about to head into the house).

gulp

———

Julian spent the next few nights sleeping in the shed, surviving on nuts, berries and guinea-pig food. The Man-up Survival weekend hadn't been a complete waste of time after all.

21

Disappearing Acts

I didn't see Sandy for days. I even found myself looking for him like he used to look for me.

I stood outside his block of flats and texted him, and even put a **kiss**.

to: SANDY
Sorry I was mean x

But he didn't answer. I checked to see if it was in my sent messages. Maybe he'd got no credit? I told Mum I felt bad.

Not as bad as I feel about my polystyrene tiles.

Then she told me that she'd seen Sandy at the shopping centre with his mum. His dad was (very  in hospital.)

'Oh, no! Poor Sandy!'

She said Sandy was helping out because his mum was very tired and worried.

'Such a nice boy.'

'Not too nice then?' I said meaningfully. Mum was always saying Julian was too nice.

'No! Don't be silly, Jelly. And a credit to his mum.'

Then Dot, who was round drinking wine, said,

'Ere, Sue... . . . Jules is going somewhere.

Did Sandy ask about me?

What's the silly old fart up to now?

'I don't understand it,' I whimpered. 'I've said sorry!'

'Men are very unforgiving,' Dot said.

'That's a generalisation, Dot. Julian is **VERY** forgiving.'

'He'd have to be, living with you, Sue!'

And they both ꞏcꞏaꞏcꞏkꞏlꞏeꞏdꞏ like witches with **lung disease**.

'What's he doing now, Dot?' Mum asked.

'He's coming this way.'

'I knew he wouldn't last.'

'He's . . . oh, no, he's stopped. He's taking his underpants off . . .'

'Wha-a-t?!' ₒₒₒ o

'Off the <u>washing</u> line . . . going back to the shed . . .'

144

'He's packing to come back,' Mum said.

How could the subject have changed so ~~quickly~~ from Sandy and his dad, and me and **my** feelings, to Mum and Julian?

'Are you sure Sandy didn't ask about me, Mum?' I asked. 'Maybe I could cheer him u—'

'Oh, hold on, Sue,' Dot interrupted. 'He's come out, with his suitcase! Ah, bless, it keeps falling on its side and he's having to drag it . . .'

'He's coming back!' Mum cried.

I found myself **looking** forward to Julian coming back from the shed. At least he listened, even though he did smell of patchouli oil and say 'I hear you' — at least he **DID** hear me!

I went out to welcome him back, but he just gave me a brief hug, handed me a **LETTER** and *trundled* off into the night.

When I came back in Mum was doing this —

La, la-la, laaaa . . . .

CAKE MIX

. . . **STIRRING** (packet) cake mix, with her hair **UP** and an apron on, all casual and occupied, with the 'smell' of -FRESH- flowers and **just**-brewed coffee . . .

She turned with a fake look of surprise,

> Julian! You startled me!
> Where have you been?

Her face dropped when she saw it was me.

QUITE a LOT

'Julian's gone, Mum. He gave me this to give you.'

I handed her the envelope. She tore it open, read it and then ~~LITERALLY~~ collapsed on the floor ~~sobbing~~. It was quite scary. Even Fatty was alarmed.

Julian! **Julian!**

But then Fatty noticed some cake mix on her fingers and started to lick it . . .

'Get off, Fatty!' Mum screamed. 'It's all your fault! Julian's **ALLERGIC** to you and you peed on his lavender bush! And **KILLED** it!'

I read the note while Mum continued wailing and blaming Fatty, who was otherwise engaged licking out the mixing bowl.

Sue,

I AM LEAVING TO GO BACK AND LIVE WITH ANTHEA. YOU AND I, I REALISE, AREN'T COMPATIBLE AND I'M NOT HAPPY.

ANTHEA ACCEPTS ME FOR WHO I AM, A 'WEAK', 'SPINELESS', 'BORING', 'HOPELESS EXCUSE FOR A MAN' (TO QUOTE YOU).

AND I ACCEPT ANTHEA FOR WHO SHE IS, A 'DULL', 'HUMOURLESS', 'SKINNY' 'EMBARRASSMENT TO WOMANKIND' (TO QUOTE YOU AGAIN).

REGARDS
JULIAN

'I never said "skinny",' Mum wailed. 'I said "shapeless"!'

Three hours later the note was crumpled and damp with tears.

Mum was clutching it in the armchair, with me, Dot, Jay, Fatty and Cat all sitting round her, trying to still look interested.

Mmm, really . . .

'He didn't even put "Dear Sue". Just "Sue"! So cold. And no kiss! He never ever doesn't put a kiss,' she said for the 193rd time.

My brother **cracked**,

Mum, face it, Julian is gone!

There's plenty more wet fish in the sea!

'It's only been two hours!' she cried.

we all reminded her.

'Just move on, Mum,' Jay said.

'Don't be so heartless, Jay!'

'That's what you said to me when Kelly Harris dumped me . . .'

Mum stared at Jay with her glacé-cherry eyes.

'Julian has **NOT** dumped me! He's trying to -SCARE- me, isn't he, Dot?'

'Definitely,' Dot agreed.

But Mum threw herself on the floor wailing again, anyway.

22

Stiff Competition

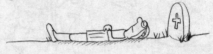

Although I'd convinced myself I did actually win the school CROSS COUNTRY. I thought maybe I should put in a weeny bit of training before the county championship. It was partly because when I ran a few paces to the kitchen to get a digestive biscuit during a commercial break I couldn't really breathe...

I persuaded Myf and Roobs to come for a run with me, but then Mum asked if SHE could come too. Ever since Julian had gone back to Anthea Mum had got very **Clingy**. She wanted to hang out with me ALL the time.

'Julian might be in the park!' she cried.

Pathetic, I thought.

Even though **I'd** thought **Sandy** might be in the park.

And then I thought: Maybe Sandy will come and watch the cross country? He came to all my other sporting events.

We did quite a fast lap round the park. Mum was the opposite of a pace setter — we were running **away** from her and her embarrassing track suit,

Julian this . . . Julian that . . .
Don't you think, Jelly? Jelleeee!

. . . but it was mainly her droning ON and ON and **ON** about Julian that kept us

going (he is her NEW ADDICTION).

When we got home we saw Fatty's head appearing and reappearing above the fence towards the washing line.

'Julian's sock!' Mum cried. 'He might come back for it. It's hard to find those loose-topped ones in natural fibre!'

But that wasn't what Fatty was after. He was jumping up, over and over again, trying to get to the half a coconut Mum had put out for Julian's wild birds.

'Well at least he's getting some exercise, silly fool,' Mum said.

The next day, the day of the CROSS COUNTRY, I went to get out of bed but nothing would move. My WHOLE body had gone *dead* like my arm sometimes goes when Fatty sleeps on it.

'Fatty?' I croaked. He must be on my back, I thought, and that's why I can't move.

It was strange, as he usually licked my face in the morning asking for his breakfast.

Eventually I managed to slide out of bed and drag myself to the top of the stairs... I was Stiff! Stiff from running! That was it — I'd used muscles I hadn't used for years (i.e. all of them, except facial ones).

Then I saw Fatty at the bottom of the stairs!

He was walking with his front legs, and dragging his back legs behind him.

Jumping up at the coconut for seven and a half hours had temporarily paralysed his back legs.

I managed to slide down the stairs on my bum and found I could walk as long as I didn't bend my arms or legs.

Fatty didn't seem to notice his back legs weren't working and just did his normal fat dog behaviour:

begging while I ate my breakfast,

trying to jump up and down when I knocked his lead,

and trying to chase Cat down the garden.

Mum wasn't **Stiff** at all.

It's because I've got excellent BMI and flexibility, giuseppe says . . .

Then she turned on me . . .

Don't mention that man's name in this house! He's the reason Julian left!

There were lots of +PLUS+ points to being stiff as opposed to bendy.

1) I couldn't do anything.

Including –

a) Take Fatty out (for a drag)

b) Be Jay's slave

c) DO THE CROSS COUNTRY – WHICH WAS TODAY !!!!!!!!

I got texts from Myf and Roobs that said . . .

ROOBS
Paralysed from the neck down. May not live x

MYF
I CAN'T WALK!!! ☺

I'd just manoeuvred myself on to the sofa to watch telly (my eyes weren't **stiff** at least) when the doorbell ʀᴀɴɢ.

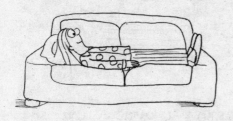

'Darling!' my mum called. 'It's Mrs . . . Fish . . . or whatever her name is . . . come to take you to the cross country!'

'**Haddock**. And it's **Miss**, actually,' Miss Haddock told her. 'Ah, Jellifer. Come along. Get your kit on!'

But I can't move, Miss.

Why not, Jellifer?

I'm *stiff from running.*

Nonsense, Jellifer – best thing for stiff muscles is exercise . . .

She's right, Jells, that's what giuseppe . . .

Mum's expression <u>changed</u> and she yelled at me and Miss Haddock –

Don't mention that man's name in this house!

Mum had to dress me and put me in my 'lucky' wellies (humiliating). And I had to be slid on to the back seat of Miss Haddock's car (more humiliating - a few neighbours gathered to watch).

But if I thought **THAT** was humiliating, I'd obviously led a very sheltered life. This cross country wasn't done through allotments and woods – it was a 5,000m race ROUND a TRACK and ...

1) Röger Lövely was there watching, because he was doing the long jump later.

2) I came completely last in the cross country and was so slow that I was still on the track for the next few races and managed to come last in those as well.

3) After all that I was <u>**DISQUALIFIED**</u> for wearing wellies.

Thank GOD Sandy wasn't there.

Roger Lovely was really sweet afterwards and offered to pull off my wellies which **STANK**, but then I saw him **kiss** Amy George,

our star sprinter — well, he <u>DID</u> say he liked sporty girls and I wasn't sporty, though I couldn't help feeling I was **QUITE** a good sport . . .

. . . and anyway he was boring and **THICK** compared to Sandy. It was only his looks that were interesting . . .

Distracting hair

Absorbing nose

Mesmerising ears

Fascinating eyelashes

Entertaining shoulders

Thought-provoking lips

23

Facial Hair

Of course, it would have to be then, wouldn't it? When I saw Sandy for the first time at school for weeks. Myf had brought in her set of false moustaches. We'd already used the stink bombs on Mr Bucket and the whoopee cushion on Miss Haddock, who'd sat on it and broken it before it could let off a real Bronx cheer.

We'd promised to do a trick on every teacher before the end of the day and it was the last lesson of the day. Yes, double biology with my favourite teacher Miss Jasmine, who hated me even when my face was clean-shaven.

The challenge was this:

Miss Jasmine had to actually **see** each of us in 3 different moustaches by the end of the lesson.

We'd done it with Ms Dimmock in art with silly faces and she hadn't even noticed . . .

Now, girls, three quick sketches of Cicily in one-minute poses, OK?

She was too busy looking for a new job in the Guardian.

But of course Miss Jasmine noticed straight away.

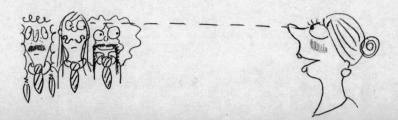

Well, she noticed **ME** anyway and called me up in front of the class.

She said in a **VERY LOUD** voice,

'Jelly, please explain the facial hair.'

It's a moustache, Miss Jasmine.

. . .just as Sandy walked past the window.

I tried to wave to him but, well, he probably didn't recognise me in my **'Sheriff's Curl'**.

24

Cool Girl Out In the Cold

Myf, Roobs and I were at the shopping centre doing 'h̲a̲n̲g̲i̲n̲g̲ o̲u̲t̲' when I spotted Bethany sitting on a seat all alone looking sad.

Kiera and Jade aren't speaking to me any more because Kiera is going out with Billy and they say I'm not mature because . . . I let out some . . . gas . . . at your party. Which I didn't.

'You can hang out with us!' I told her. 'You could join our 𝒞𝐿𝒰𝐵.'

We're always letting out gas!

— Not always.

Bethany made me feel very silly when she entered our headquarters/my bedroom and said,

Ooooh **Pink!**

in a very patronising way. At first she was very obedient and Faithful and agreed to **all** the Faithful Club rules —

But then she stared to subtly change the rules. She made us play a game called 'Family'.

Let's all be a family! I'll be Mum.

She told Myf she was her true daughter but that I was an adopted sea slug and that Rubi was an adopted old potato.

Roobs and I were a little uneasy about our roles in the family but we were so surprised that cool girls played silly games that we went along with it.

On Sunday Bethany insisted we meet at her house and her bedroom wasn't *Pink!*, it was VERY COOL . . .

Bethany's Room

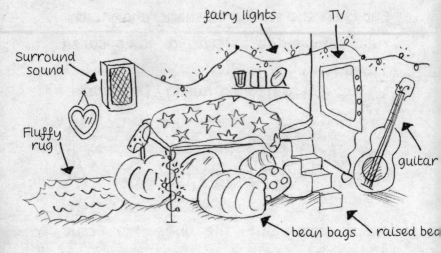

fairy lights

TV

Surround sound

Fluffy rug

guitar

bean bags

raised bed

All day at school during break we played Family, but **THEN** one lunchtime before school dinners, Bethany said that I wasn't invited to the family lunch.

So I spent lunchtime in the library with Audrey Tharp who didn't **lOOK** up from her Harry Potter book once.

The next day I **Steeled** myself for rejection but Bethany was all smiles. This time she excluded Myf from a family trip to the seaside (girls' toilets).

And the next day she excluded Rubi but

included Ricky, who had **NO** idea **WHAT** was going on (boy).

Rubi said it was 'Divide and Rule' – which means you turn all the members of the club against each other so you can have control over them <u>all</u>. We Secretly agreed to throw Bethany out of the F.C. but we were too "scared" to tell her and she had a way of staring at you with burning eyes . . .

. . . which befuddled you and put you right off.

The others said I had to tell her because I had invited her to join. But when I tried to speak to her (in a "shaky" sheep's voice) she went all Smiley and gooey and said she had a secret to tell me and did I want half her Maltesers, and to borrow her nail varnish? She **REALLY** only wanted to be in a club with me — Rubi, Myf and Ricky were so *immature*! Did I want to go to her house for tea? Did I want to be best friends? He, he, he, he, he, he   Etc. etc.

I resisted — which took a *LOT* of willpower, I can tell you.

But **NOT** enough to ask her to leave.

Cling On, Mum

Bethany kept **shOwing Off** that she was allowed two weeks off school to stay with her dad and his girlfriend in Majorca.

Majorca this.
Majorca that.
Sea. Suntan
Spanish boys.

We were all very relieved when she left.

We could get back to a **democracy** instead of a **dictatorship** – or so we thought.

Roobs, Myf and I started excitedly deciding what we would do while she was away – hoping that she wouldn't come back – when Mum barged into the room.

'Hi, girls, mind if I join you?'

And that was **IT**.

She wanted to join in with everything we were doing.

She came to the cinema with us . . .

What did she say? Can't make head
nor tail of it. What's going on!?
Who's that blonde girl?

Shhh!

She came shopping with us . . .

Wait up, gang! Which one?
Julian loves me in miniskirts!

Jell, you've got to
ditch your mum.

She even came to Ellie Smith's party with us . . .

I just didn't appreciate him, Mike.

And bored her dad about Julian.

If I suggested maybe she find some friends of her **OWN** age or go to the museums (on her **own**, like she suggests to **me** if **I'm** bored) she did this –

Fine! You go off and enjoy yourself with your friends. Me and Cat will be fine all on our own, won't we, Cat? Don't worry about me (sniff) . . . or Cat.

Or she did this –

And then I'd do this –

Oh, come on then . . .

Great, let me get my jacket!

Totally forgetting Cat, of course →

She was a (ling·on Julian bore.

I was considering giving myself up for adoption one day when a postcard pl̂ôpped on to the mat. It read –

Dear Sea Slug,
How's it going, Fatty?
(Only joking.) You smell.
(Where's your sense of humour?!) Miss you. Not!
Back on Sunday. Get the popcorn in – none for you though, lardybum (joking!)
Your bessy mate, Bethany x (NOT!)

JELLY ROWNTREE
22 RIDGEWELL RD
SE6
UK

Jelly →

My heart ♥ ♥ ♥ sank.

But then, 'Girls! Girls!' my mum shouted up from the living room. 'Let's do a play! I'll be director!'

Yes! Yes! That was it – there was no way Bethany would stay in a gang with a mum in it! I told Myf and Roobs . . . .

Just wait it out till she sees Mum, then we can get rid of her.

Great idea! Get rid of who?

They might get on . . .

–26–

Queen Mum

Roobs was right. Mum was the only one that Bethany didn't try to boss about or exclude. They became as thick as thieves.

Let's play Beauty Parlour! I'll be the boss, you can be the assistant!

OK, Sue.

'You two can be our customers. Jelly, you're the cleaner,' she told us.

You look gorgeous, girls!

Back to your ugly old selves!

One day Mum tried to exclude Bethany from a game of Orphans and they had a burny-eyed stare out.

Bethany ⟹stormed out crying and Mum put the rest of us in a cupboard, including Fatty, for being naughty orphans.

But unfortunately Mum made up with Bethany the next day.

Hi, Bethywethany!
Fancy a girly shopping outing?
I won't invite the others.

Myf and Roobs started to make pathetic excuses not to come round and happily excluded themselves from all forthcoming fake events –

I'm helping my dad worm the dog.

 I can't find my shoes.

So I was left in the Bethany-and-Mum club.

 I'm the Queen, Bethany's the Princess and Jelly's the jester! Entertain us, jester! Or else!

One day Mum was favouring Bethany and

excluding me. They were playing prison guards (watching TV).

Masterchef is Julian's favourite programme.

Billy likes—

He's a very good cook, and washer-upper.

181

I was happily sitting in my room (cell).
I texted Myf and Roobs, and even Ricky,
who even though he didn't know what
was going on, had also stopped coming
round – but **NO ONE** answered. I was
trapped in the Bethany-and-Mum club
with no rules!

I put on some sad music
and looked at old pictures
of the Faithful Club.
I came across one
of the roses
that Sandy

had given me pressed in my
photo album, when Mum
walked in (the other prison
guard had gone home in a **HUFF**).

'You are released from prison . . .' she
announced. 'What's that? Ah, is it one of
the roses that Sandy gave you, darling?'

'Give it back!' I yelled at her.

'So you still like him then', she said, sitting on my bed, and managing to **drag** a brain cell away from herself and Julian.

'No, I just feel guilty that I was so horrible.'

'Oh, I know what you mean.' (She was already weeping.) 'I feel so bad about the way I treated Julian, I didn't appreciate . . .'

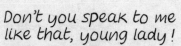

OH SHUT UP!

I'm trying to talk! And you just keep going on about Julian — it's all me, me, me with you!

Don't you speak to me like that, young lady!

You're so bossy and selfish. No wonder he left!

Mum did her raging-bull face and I ran out of the front door and slammed it just in time.

I was storming along, slightly regretting not stopping to get my phone or purse, when I saw JULIAN *loping* down the high street. He was unshaven, his hair was ASKEW and he was still wearing Mum's 'jumper' which was FILTHY and had a cheese-and-onion crisp packet hanging off the back of it. Julian NEVER ate hydrogenated FAT!

He hugged me really **tight**. He was a bit smelly but at least there was a crisp left in the packet which I ate to mask the SMELL.

Jelly!

How's your mother?

Very boring. How's Anthea?

 Anthea wouldn't take me back. She said I was a 'wet, spineless, boring, hapless excuse for a man' and she wasn't quoting your mother.

No because Mum said 'hopeless' not 'hapless'.

Hmmm, well anyway, don't tell your mother but I've been staying at my mother's, but she says I'm under her feet — so I'm going to get a bedsit. Don't tell your mother.

Don't worry, I won't. I'll let her suffer.

'Suffer?' Julian cried, 'You mean . . . ?'

'Ye-es,' I admitted. 'She misses you — but she's not worth it, Julian. You deserve better.'

'I don't!' Julian insisted. 'I worship the ground she stomps on.'

What shall I do, Jelly?

Let her ◦sweat◦ for at least another hour. Then she'll be so grateful to have you back she won't find you annoying for at least a week.

'A whole week! That would be wonder-ful,' he exclaimed.

'And keep the stubble, she'll like that.'

Then Julian took me for a hot chocolate and I told him all about how I'd been mean to Sandy and now I was sorry, but I hadn't seen him and now I realised I liked him, even though he was SHORT.

Julian said, 'Tell him you like him. What have you got to lose but your pride? And who lies on their deathbed wishing they had a bit more pride?'

We both went QUIet, thinking that possibly Mum would.

⸘THANKGOD⸘ Julian was back – Mum made him beg – it's like she TRIES to make him annoying. He did at least refuse to get on his knees and KISS her Ugg boots.

The house smelt of patchouli again, and Mum left our gang and rejoined Julian's gang.

27

Nut Allergy

Unfortunately I was still **STUCK** with Bethany, and Myf and Roobs were still refusing to come round until I'd got rid of her. But she was getting more and **more** bossy in more and more subtle ways.
We would walk along the road and she'd suddenly s l o w down, so I had to slow down.

Or she would ≡speed up, so I had to speed up to keep up with her.

If I pointed this out, she had a burny-eyed, smiley way of making me feel like I was mad and imagining things.

One day I saw Myf, Roobs and Ricky on the other side of the high street playing in a GIANT cardboard box. I was just about to call out to them but Bethany linked my arm and said,

God, look at those losers.

They looked like they were having lots of FUN, and I felt all empty Bethany had confused and exhausted me by blowing

 and **COLD**

and then hypnotised me into thinking I only needed one friend – HER.

Bethany started saying horrible things like 'Your mum's a nutter' and 'Your stepdad's a weirdo.' And 'Your dog's obese'!

(Only I was allowed to say things like that about my family.)

But if I took offence she'd link my arm and say, 'Only joking, sea slug!' and lend me her **iPod**, or **lipgloss** or let me wear her **boots with high heels**.

She'd say,

'Let's throw water bombs at people,'

or, 'Let's knock on old ladies' doors and run away,'

or, 'Let's phone people up and blow raspberries down the phone.'

Sitting on a wall one day she was pelting people with peanuts and then looking **innocent**, when she clunked Chez – who had appeared out of Claire's Accessories – with a particularly large one.

ooh!

Oi!

shouted Chez.

'It was her!' Bethany, my loyal friend, shouted back, pointing at me.

'Nah, it weren't! Jez is our mate. She helped us come third in the cross country and make our mums proud of us and give us money to spend in Claire's.'

I bought this hair toggle, but it's already broke!

Shuddup, Kaz!

What you gonna do about it, BEZ?

'Bez' looked genuinely SCARED – a look I hadn't seen before – and her eyes went watery.

'Nothing,' she said in a very small voice, and slid off the wall and walked away, speeding up as she went. And this time

I didn't have to try to keep up.

'She been bovverin' you, Jez?' Kaz asked, putting her big arm round me protectively.

'A bit,' I told her.

'If you bovva Jez again, you'll 'ave us to answer to!!' Chez shouted after Bethany, who broke into a run and disappeared round the corner.

'You wanna join our gang, Jells? We're going to Wez's to practise hair straightening?' Kaz enquired.

That was REALLY kind of them but I told them my hair was already straight.

I said my goodbyes and rushed round to see Myf and Roobs. I was so happy to see them! And later on we went to mine and played baby left on the doorstep with Fatty (**don't** tell anyone).

28

Missing the Beat

Myf and Roobs said Sandy hadn't been at rehearsals much but they thought he was still playing in the concert.

Obviously I was going to the school concert anyway to support Myf and Roobs (someone had to) but it would be my chance to talk to Sandy at the after concert party.

My heart skipped a little beat when I saw the keyboards, but it wasn't Sandy playing, it was some girl. I felt really

disappointed and was only moment-
arily distracted by Myf's and Roobs'
tambourine and maracas solos.

Myf hit Cicily on the head with her
tambourine (good) and Roobs got
confuzed and hit herself in the
face with her maraca
(unfortunate).

*I might have given
myself brain
damage.*

But they weren't bad at all – just a bit
embarrassing and stiff.

But when it came to Angel Farraday's
triangle solo I could see what Mr Bucket
meant about playing with `·'''PaSSion'·`.

She played with her eyes closed, smiling and tapping her feet and swirling about.

It was mesmerising! The whole audience was captivated by her.

The after concert party was really crowded and we were SQUASHED up against the drinks table (quite useful).

SLURP

Someone behind me said, 'Hi, Sandy . . .' but when I looked round I couldn't see him. Then a voice from above said, 'Hello, Jelly!'

I looked up . . .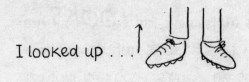

And up . . .

And up . . .

SANDY
BLATCH!

His hair was different, his **lOOKS** had improved and he'd done what my mum said he might do – he'd shot up! Now he really looked like B.B.!

That you up there, Sandy?

The most popular girl in the school was eyeing him up. The 137th most popular girl in the school, Myfanwy, said,

Look, Jelly! Sandy's all tall! You can go out with him now!

Shut UP, Myfanwy, you *stupid, stupid* . . .

. . . that's what I **wanted** to say (and do).
But I said . . .

and Sandy said,

I think we discovered in no
uncertain terms that Jelly
really doesn't want to.

'No, Sandy, Jelly just thought you were
too short and a bit creepy but now you're
all tall and a bit cool,' Myf said.

'I'm really not cool,' laughed Sandy.

I put my hands over Myf's mouth.

No, that's not it at all.

mm..
mm
mm

and I was just about to continue . . .

'I don't care if you're short or not, and you weren't creepy — I just like you. There, I've said it.'

. . . when Sandy interrupted (thank heavens) and said,

'Hey, no worries. I was a little twerp — I was going through a bad time and was a bit of a cling-on — but I've got a new girlfriend now. We got together a few months ago — yes, when I was an annoying little twerp! She was very supportive when my dad was ill. Great to see you, Jell, Myf . . . bye.'

 Ooh-er, Jelly, it's Angel Farraday.

He was **SO** nice! And he'd been **SO** nice to me! And now he was being nice to Angel Farraday! I was jealous.

We all went back to mine after the concert and I couldn't stop thinking about Sandy.

Rubi said (her auntie's a psychotherapist),

 You didn't feel you deserved someone being nice to you because you have low self-worth.

and Myf said,

You didn't feel like you deserved to go out with someone short and creepy.

Mum said,

 You never know what you've got
till it's gone.

And Julian said,

That's very true,
Susan, but you
were lucky because
I came back.

And Mum said,

Oh shut up, Julian.
I always knew
you'd come back.

Jay said,

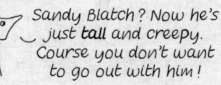 Sandy Blatch? Now he's
just **tall** and creepy.
Course you don't want
to go out with him!

And Mum said,

> Maybe you just want him to like
> you, rather than you liking him?

> Maybe that's you
> and Julian you're
> talking about.

Not at all. I love Julian.

Then Julian wandered into the kitchen
eating an apple. Mum said,

> For goodness sake, Julian, eat
> it with your mouth closed!

Phew. Everything was back to normal.

29

No More Miss Embarrassed Girl

I went to bed that night feeling relieved. I didn't even mind Fatty (growling) when I moved my leg.

Grrr . . .

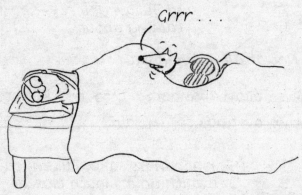

He was the only boyfriend I wanted for now. It wasn't that I felt envious of Sandy and Angel because I wanted to be Sandy's girlfriend. It's because I want to be more like them. I am SICK of being an **embarrassed** person.

Sandy and Angel aren't embarrassed or
scared . . .

Sandy declared his love for me,

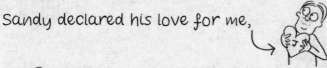

argued with scary boys
wearing only one boot,

played the keyboards,
swaying not Stiff,

went shopping with his
mum linking arms

and forgave me with a smile,

And Angel is the same.

She hugs her mum outside the school gates,

 plays the triangle with passion,

squares up to scary girls pretending to be a martial arts expert →

Hi-i-i-Ya!

 and was super friendly to me even though she knows I was Sandy's first choice.

BUT I found EVERYTHING **embarrassing**!

E.g.

When Sandy
loved me

When Roger
was near

coo ee!

When Mum met
me from school

When I
played the
triangle

When I
won the
cross
country

When Fatty pooed
in the middle of
the high street
(understandable)

People really only care if they make
fools of themselves — if it's someone else
they're just thankful and relieved it's
not them. So really it was a kindness to
others to make a fool of yourself, if you
thought about it.

I made up my mind that I would do **three** things the next day that deep down I wanted to do but which could very likely cause **embarrassment**.

1) Wear a brightly coloured hat that I liked but which drew attention to myself.
2) Wear my Faithful Club badge (the extra-large one).
3) Refuse to be Jay's slave any more.

So the next day I did the first two things.

I walked tall-ish and no one even looked my way!

Well, Billy Rumble glanced my way, but I had perfected my burny-eyed smile and he just looked at his feet.

Billy Rumble was supposedly a cool boy, but Kiera had dumped him and I noticed him standing about on his own quite a lot, sneering at people.

School orchestra? That's for wimps.

School play? That's for losers.

Girlfriends? That's for . . . girls!

He might be cool, but he wasn't very nice and he didn't look at all happy. Later on after school I saw him having a sneaky look at the advert for kids to join the after-school Chess Club,

but then he saw me and muttered,

Chess? That's for girly, wimpy losers who play chess!

Then for the third thing that would possibly cause **embarrassment**: refusing to be Jay's slave any more (yes, I was still employed in that capacity, when his one brain cell remembered).

I decided that if **Röger Lövely** found out I liked him, so what? He'd be flattered and I'd be 'sweet'.

Plate of sweet and savouries, Jelly. Now!

No.

I beg your pardon?

<u>N O</u> spells NO.

Right, well, in that case, I'm going to . . . what was it?

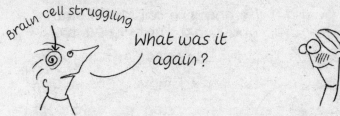

Brain cell struggling

What was it again?

I felt myself begin to blush but held firm.

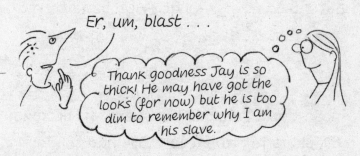

Er, um, blast . . .

Thank goodness Jay is so thick! He may have got the looks (for now) but he is too dim to remember why I am his slave.

What was it? I'm losing my mind . . .

While he was in a weak position I decided to

COUNTER ATTACK!

I'm going to tell Mum I saw you smoking at my party.

(I hadn't.)

Did you? When? Oh please don't, Jell. I don't even smoke!

JAY is S C A R E D of Mum.

Grrr!

eek!

So I said I wouldn't tell her if he became MY slave for two weeks. He had to:

1) Tell me **FAT CAT** and **THIN MIN** stories at bedtime like he used to.

2) Take Myf and Roobs on a triple date to the pictures to see *Princesses in Love* and kiss them both on the cheek afterwards.

3) Rub my feet.

4) Give me complete control of the remote.

But, best of all,

5) Take Fatty on all walks, as at that
moment he was wearing a lampshade
on his head to stop him eating himself.

Hur!

Hur!

Hur, hur,
stupid hat.

30

Girl's Best Friend

Well, it was Saturday morning and I was feeling a bit sorry for myself.

Mum and Julian were giggling over breakfast, Jay and Carla were sunbathing in the garden. I expected Sandy and Angel were doing a ♪musical♫ duet somewhere, Bethany, Kiera and Jade were probably pelting people with nuts at the shopping centre, and Roger and Amy were no doubt being sporty together.

Anyway, I thought to myself, I've still got Fatty . . .

and I've still got Buster Bauble.

And I could share him with Myf and Roobs (and 3 million other silly girls, and Ricky).

So I phoned Myf and Roobs and invited them round for a Faithful Club meeting. We were going to try to save enough money to get tickets to see O.M.G. in concert in the spring. But how . . . ?

We decided to think about it later, and played Cats Play Monopoly instead (DON'T tell anyone).

Miaow!

Purr!

Maaaheoww . . .

Jelly thinks she <u>should</u> be cool but knows deep down she isn't – and that her friends Myf and Roobs definitely aren't.

This is me aged 11.
Like Jelly, I wasn't very cool . . .

Rob 'Bobert' Hopf
(my Ricky Chin)

. . . but the bobble hat added an air of sophistication, I feel.

Up until Big School the idea of being cool never occurred to me . . . but then for a while I thought I <u>should</u> be cool (i.e. be like everyone else) and was a bit mean to my nice, loyal friends, who were a bit different, and too nice to the cool, mature girls, who were all the same and who I didn't even really like.

I quickly realised though that maturity is overrated . . .

and that it's more important to be warm than cool.

Thank Yous

A giant thank you to everyone at Macmillan, especially my editor Rachel Petty for her invaluable guidance, Rachel Vale for the 'zingy' cover and chats about Danish drama (tak), and the incomparable Tracey Ridgewell, the designer (who's 'never worked so long' on a book), for her never-ending patience, witty turn of phrase and KitKats.

An extra giant thank you to Veronique Baxter, who encouraged me to write these books and who is my friend as well as my agent.

And the giantest thank you of all to my husband Robin, who has laughed long and loudly at this book, even though he is not an 11-year-old girl (and he did the handwriting font for me too), and my wonderful stepdaughters Rosie, Heather and Robin Shaw for being all-round marvellous and reminding me about being 12.